Classic Collection

ALICE'S ADVENTURES IN WONDERLAND

LEWIS CARROLL

Adapted by Ronne Randall • Illustrated by Robert Dunn

QED Publishing

Down the Rabbit Hole

It was a hot summer's day, and Alice was sitting with her sister on the riverbank. She was beginning to get very tired. Once or twice she peeped over at the book her sister was reading. There were no pictures in it, none at all, and just looking at the pages made Alice feel sleepy…

All at once, a very strange sight made Alice sit up and stare. A White Rabbit with pink eyes was running right past her – and he was dressed in a jacket and waistcoat, carrying a little rolled-up umbrella! Even stranger, the rabbit pulled a golden watch out of his waistcoat pocket, and said to himself (in a very worried voice), "Oh, dear! Oh, dear! I shall be too late!"

Alice jumped to her feet and ran after the rabbit, catching up with him just in time to see him pop down a large hole under a hedge.

Of course, Alice scrambled down the hole after him, and found herself tumbling down a long, dark well. It seemed that she would never stop falling, when suddenly – *thump!* – down she came upon a heap of sticks and dry leaves.

When Alice looked around, she found she was in a long hallway. Up ahead of her was the White Rabbit, still fretting about being late. There were little doors all round the hall, but they were all locked. Alice began to wonder how she would ever get out.

Suddenly, Alice came upon a three-legged table with a tiny golden key on it. She tried the key in every door, then noticed a curtain with a little door behind it. It was just the right size for the golden key!

Alice opened the door, and on the other side she saw the loveliest garden anyone could imagine. She longed to go through and explore the garden. But she was much too big to fit through the doorway.

She went back to the table, in case there was a key for another door, but she only found a small bottle. Its label said 'DRINK ME'. Alice knew enough not to do that! She thought, "I'll look first, to see if it says 'POISON' anywhere!" When she found that it didn't, she drank some of what was in the bottle. Instantly, strange things began to happen.

"What a curious feeling!" Alice said to herself. "I must be shutting up like a telescope!" Smaller and smaller she grew, until she was only ten inches tall. She rushed to the little door – but she had left the key on the table, and now she was too small to reach it!

Alice was about to cry when she spied a little glass box under the table. Inside was a cake with the words 'EAT ME' spelled out in currants. Alice ate the cake, eager to see what would happen next.

"Curiouser and curiouser!" she exclaimed. "Now I'm opening out like the largest telescope that ever was!" Taller and taller she grew, until – *bump!* – her head hit the ceiling.

The Pool of Tears

Poor Alice was further from the garden than ever. All she could do was peer through the doorway with one eye. Feeling hopeless, she burst into tears. She cried gallons of tears, until a pool four inches deep surrounded her.

She then saw the White Rabbit hurrying along with a pair of gloves in one hand and a fan in the other. "Oh, the Duchess!" he was muttering. When he saw Alice he dropped the fan and gloves and scurried off.

Alice picked them up, and, as the hall was very hot, she began to fan herself. "Oh, I feel so strange," she said. "Now I seem to be swimming in the sea!" But as she looked around she saw that the 'sea' was actually her own tears. She had shrunk again! She dropped the fan at once.

Alice splashed about until she saw something in the distance. She swam towards it, thinking it must be a walrus. Then she remembered how small she was, and realized it was only a Mouse.

"Excuse me, Mouse," she said politely, "do you know the way out?"

The Mouse did not answer, so Alice thought it might not understand English. "I'll try speaking French," she thought. But the only words she could remember were *Où est ma chatte?* which means "Where is my cat?" This made the Mouse jump with fright.

Alice apologized to the Mouse, and promised she would not mention cats again. But the Mouse was angry.

"Cats are horrible things," he said, swimming away.

While Alice was trying to talk to the Mouse, the pool had been filling up with other creatures, and now it was quite crowded. There was a Duck, a Dodo, a Lory, an Eaglet and several other birds. Suddenly, Alice noticed they were outside. The water must have washed them out! They swam to the edge of the pool to try and work out how to get dry.

The Mouse tried making a dry, boring speech, but this didn't work, so the Dodo suggested they have a race. By the time they'd finished running, everyone was dry – but then they all began to quarrel about who had won the race. Luckily, Alice found a tin of sweets in her pocket, so she settled the argument by giving everyone a sweet as a prize.

When things had calmed down, the Mouse began to tell a long and sad tale about how he came to hate cats so much. But, without meaning to, Alice upset him again by starting to talk about her own cat. He ran off.

"I wish Dinah were here," Alice sighed. "She would fetch him back again."

"Who is Dinah?" asked one of the birds.

"She is my cat," Alice replied, "and she is very good at catching mice!"

At the mention of the word 'cat', all the birds became very alarmed and rushed off, leaving Alice alone again.

The Rabbit Sends in Bill

Alice wasn't alone for long. Just a few minutes later, the White Rabbit came trotting along, still muttering to himself. "The Duchess!" he fretted. "Oh, my dear paws! Oh, my fur and whiskers! Where can I have dropped them?"

Alice guessed that he was looking for the fan and gloves. She started looking for them, but they were nowhere to be found. In fact, everything had changed since she had been in the pool of tears. She was standing in front of a little house, with a nameplate that said 'W. RABBIT'.

As soon as the White Rabbit noticed Alice, he asked her to go into the house and fetch a fan and a pair of gloves. Alice did as he asked, and found the fan and gloves on a table. But just as she was about to leave, she noticed something peculiar. The house seemed to be getting smaller and smaller...

Actually, Alice was getting bigger! Soon she was so big that she had to crouch down to keep from getting squashed. A minute later she had to lie down and put her arms out of the windows and one leg up through the chimney!

The White Rabbit stomped up to the house. He was very cross that Alice was stuck inside. There was no room to get in the door because Alice's knee was in the hallway. He tried to climb in through the window, but that didn't work either, as he kept falling down. At last he called his gardener, Pat, to help him try and get Alice out.

Pat fetched two ladders and a Lizard called Bill, whom he ordered about. Pat and Bill tied the ladders together and tried to get to the top window.

Meanwhile, a group of animals had gathered to gawk at the giant stuck in the White Rabbit's house. Alice didn't like being gawked at, and liked it even less when the White Rabbit suggested burning the house down.

"If you do," Alice called, "I'll set Dinah on you!"

To herself, she thought, "If they had any sense, they'd just take the roof off."

But the roof stayed on, and Alice heard the White Rabbit say, "A barrowful will do, to begin with."

"A barrowful of what?" Alice wondered. She got her answer a moment later, when she was pelted with pebbles that were being thrown by the animals. Some of them hit her in the face, and as they did, they turned into tiny cakes. She swallowed one, and was delighted to find that she began to shrink at once.

She ate more and more of the tiny cakes, until she was small enough to get through the door. Then she made her escape.

Advice from a Caterpillar

Alice soon found herself in a thick wood. She was quite tiny by this time, and she wanted to get back to her normal size again.

"I probably have to eat or drink something," she thought, "but what?"

She couldn't see any cakes or anything to drink, but a very large mushroom was growing nearby. As she got closer, she saw a blue Caterpillar sitting on the top, smoking a curly water pipe.

"Who are you?" asked the Caterpillar.

"I'm not really sure," Alice replied. "So many strange things have happened, and I can't seem to stay the same size for very long."

"Well, what size would you like to be?" asked the Caterpillar.

"A bit larger than I am now," said Alice. "Three inches is a terrible height."

"Three inches is a very good height indeed!" said the Caterpillar, drawing himself up to his full height – which was exactly three inches tall.

"I'm sorry," said Alice. "I didn't mean to offend you!"

The Caterpillar took a puff of his water pipe and yawned. "One side will make you grow taller," he told Alice, "and the other side will make you shrink shorter."

"One side of what?" Alice wondered to herself.

"Of the mushroom," the Caterpillar replied, just as if Alice had said the words aloud. And then he vanished.

Alice looked at the mushroom, wondering which side was which. "I'll just have to try and see," she thought.

She stretched her arms around the mushroom and broke off a bit of each side. She nibbled a little of the right-hand bit first. *Zzzziiiipp!* She shrank so suddenly that her chin hit her foot!

There was barely enough room to open her mouth, but Alice managed to swallow some of the left-hand bit of the mushroom. This made her grow so tall that her head was in the treetops! Her neck was so long and bendy that a Pigeon, who had been sitting on her nest, flapped her wings and shrieked "Serpent!" at Alice. The Pigeon was terrified that Alice was going to steal the eggs from her nest. It took Alice a long time to convince the Pigeon that she was just a little girl and that the eggs were perfectly safe.

Once the Pigeon had settled down again, Alice carefully nibbled a bit of each piece of the mushroom, until she was finally back to her normal height.

"I've been so many different sizes," she said to herself, "that it feels a bit strange to be my right size again!"

But she didn't stay her right size for long. For, as she wandered through the wood, Alice came upon a tiny house, just four feet high. She wanted to go in, but of course she was too big. So she nibbled at the right-hand bit of the mushroom until she had shrunk down to nine inches – just the right size.

Pig and Pepper

A footman met Alice at the door, and told her that the house belonged to the Duchess. Alice could hear extraordinary noises behind the door – howling, sneezing and an occasional crash. The footman wasn't sure whether to let Alice in, but she just walked past him and opened the door herself.

Inside, the Duchess was holding a howling baby and sneezing loudly. The baby was sneezing, too. Alice herself began to sneeze as soon as she walked in. The only person not sneezing was the cook, who was busily stirring a big pot of soup.

"There must be too much pepper in that soup," Alice thought, sneezing once more. Then she noticed a Cat sitting on the hearth, grinning from ear to ear. He wasn't sneezing either.

"Why does your Cat grin like that?" Alice asked.

"It's a Cheshire Cat," said the Duchess, as if that explained everything. Meanwhile, the cook began throwing pots and pans at the Duchess and the baby. The Duchess didn't mind, and the baby just kept howling.

"Please be careful!" Alice shouted.

"Here!" shouted the Duchess. "You can hold it for a bit!" And she hurled the baby across the room. Alice caught it just in time, and was astonished to discover that it wasn't a baby at all, but a Pig!

Alice rushed out of the Duchess's house, holding the Pig. She set it down on the ground and watched as it trotted off into the wood.

As Alice wandered on, she was startled to see the Cheshire Cat sitting up in a tree, grinning down at her.

"Please can you tell me which way to go?" she asked.

"In that direction," said the Cat, waving its right paw, "lives a Hatter. And in that direction," he said, waving the other paw, "lives a March Hare. They're both mad. In fact, we're all mad here. I'm mad. You're mad."

"How do you know I'm mad?" Alice asked.

"You must be," said the Cheshire Cat, "or you wouldn't be here!"

And then he slowly began to fade away, leaving only his grin behind.

"Well," thought Alice, "that's very strange. I've often seen a cat without a grin, but I've never seen a grin without a cat before!"

Alice decided to visit the March Hare. She found his house easily – the chimneys were shaped like a hare's ears and the roof was thatched with fur. A table was set out in front, and the March Hare and the Hatter were having tea. Between them sat a Dormouse, fast asleep.

"No room! No room!" cried the Hare and the Hatter when they saw Alice.

This made Alice very cross. "There's plenty of room!" she declared, and sat down in an armchair at one end of the table.

A Mad Tea Party

"Have some wine," said the March Hare to Alice. But there was no wine on the table.

"It wasn't very polite of you to offer something that isn't here," said Alice.

"Well, it wasn't very polite of you to sit down without being invited!" the March Hare replied.

The Hatter interrupted with a riddle: "Why is a raven like a writing desk?"

"I believe I can guess that…" Alice began.

"Do you mean you think you can find out the answer?" the March Hare asked.

"Exactly," said Alice.

"Then say what you mean!" scolded the March Hare.

"I do," said Alice. "At least, I mean what I say, and that's the same thing."

"No it isn't," said the Hare. "You might as well say that 'I like what I get' is the same as 'I get what I like'!"

"Or," added the Dormouse sleepily, "that 'I breathe when I sleep' is the same as 'I sleep when I breathe'."

The Hatter, meanwhile, was looking at his watch. "Two days wrong!" he grumbled. "I told you butter wouldn't suit the works!"

"It was the best butter," said the Hare.

"There are crumbs in it. You shouldn't have put it in with the breadknife."

And so they bickered while Alice watched them curiously.

At last the Hare grew tired of arguing, and said, "Let's have a story from the Dormouse."

"Wake up, Dormouse!" said the Hatter and the Hare together. They pinched him from both sides, and he opened his eyes at last.

"I wasn't asleep," he said. "I heard every word you said!"

He then began a story about three girls, called Elsie, Lacie and Tillie, who lived at the bottom of a well.

"What did they live on?" asked Alice.

The Dormouse thought for a moment or two. "They lived on treacle," he finally replied.

"They couldn't have done that, you know," said Alice gently. "They'd have been very ill."

"They were very ill!" the Dormouse told her.

"Why did they live there?" Alice asked.

"It was a treacle well!" said the Dormouse.

"There's no such thing!" Alice exclaimed angrily.

"You can draw water from a water well," said the Hatter, "so you can draw treacle from a treacle well."

"Yes," said the Dormouse. "They were learning to draw. They drew all manner of things that begin with M… mouse-traps, and the moon, and memory, and muchness…"

"I don't think…" Alice began.

"Then you shouldn't talk!" scolded the Hatter.

Having had enough of his rudeness, Alice got up and left. The last she saw of the March Hare and the Hatter, they were trying to put the Dormouse into the teapot.

Painting the Roses Red

"That was the silliest tea party I've ever been to!" Alice thought to herself, making her way back into the wood. "I'll certainly never go there again!"

Suddenly, she noticed that the tree right in front of her had a door in the trunk. She went in, and found herself back in the long hall with all the doors. This time, when she saw the little key on the table, she knew exactly what to do, for she had kept some of the mushroom in her pocket. With a few nibbles, she got herself to the right size, opened the door and entered the lovely garden.

Several large rose trees stood at the entrance to the garden. Three gardeners – all of them with playing-card bodies – were busy painting the white roses on the rose trees red. Alice thought this was a very curious thing.

"Would you mind telling me," asked Alice, "why you are painting those roses?"

"This tree ought to have been a *red* rose tree," said one of the gardeners. "And we put a white one in by mistake. If the Queen finds out, we'd all have our heads cut off."

"The Queen!" cried another gardener suddenly. He and the others threw themselves flat on their faces.

Alice gazed at the royal procession. First came the soldiers, then the courtiers. The royal children followed, and then the guests, including the White Rabbit. Next came the Knave of Hearts, carrying the King's crown. Finally, at the very end, came the King and Queen of Hearts themselves.

The procession stopped in front of Alice. The Queen looked at her sternly and asked, "What's your name?"

"My name is Alice," Alice replied politely. But to herself she said, "They're only a pack of cards! I don't have to be afraid of them!"

"And who are they?" the Queen asked, pointing to the gardeners, who were still lying face down.

"How should I know?" asked Alice, surprised at her own courage. "They're no business of mine!"

The Queen turned red with rage. "Off with her head!" she screamed. "Off with her head!"

"Nonsense!" said Alice, and the Queen fell silent. The King said to her, timidly, "She is only a child, my dear."

The Queen turned away and shouted at the gardeners to get up. They instantly jumped up and began bowing to the Queen, the King, the royal children and everyone else.

"Stop it!" shrieked the Queen. "You're making me giddy! What have you been doing to this tree?"

One of the gardeners started to reply, but before he could finish, the Queen saw for herself that the roses were really white.

"Off with their heads!" she bellowed. As she marched off, three soldiers came forward to carry out her orders.

"You won't be beheaded," Alice assured the gardeners. She hid them in a large flowerpot, where the soldiers could not find them.

The Queen's Croquet Ground

When Alice caught up with the King and Queen, the Queen asked her, "Can you play croquet?"

"Yes," replied Alice.

"Come on, then!" the Queen roared. So Alice joined the procession, wondering what would happen next.

"Get to your places, everyone!" the Queen shouted, in a voice that sounded like thunder. People rushed about in all directions, tumbling over one another. A moment later, everyone was ready and the game could begin.

What a strange game it was! The ground was bumpy, the croquet balls were hedgehogs and the mallets were flamingos! The Queen's soldiers had to bend over and put their hands on the ground to make the arches.

Alice had trouble controlling her flamingo-mallet. Just as she got its neck straightened out, ready to hit the hedgehog, the flamingo twisted round to look at Alice with a puzzled expression. This made Alice laugh so much that she had to start all over again, by which time the hedgehog had unrolled itself and crawled away.

"What a difficult game!" Alice thought to herself.

Players did not wait for their turns, and quarrelled with each other over the hedgehogs. Before long, the Queen was stamping all over the croquet ground, shouting, "Off with her head!" in her loudest voice.

Alice was very worried. "What if she wants to chop off my head?" she thought with a shudder. "They're so fond of beheading people, it's a wonder anyone is still alive!"

Alice was looking for some way to escape when she noticed a curious shape, hanging in the air. After studying it for a minute or two, she realized it was a grin.

"It's the Cheshire Cat!" she said to herself. "Now at least I'll have someone to talk to!"

Soon the Cheshire Cat's whole head appeared. He was pleased to see Alice, too. "How do you like the Queen?" he asked her.

"I don't like her at all," Alice whispered. "She's so very…"

"Who are you talking to?" asked the King, coming up beside Alice and looking at the Cheshire Cat's head with great interest.

"Allow me to introduce my friend the Cheshire Cat," said Alice.

"I don't like it," said the King. "It must be removed." He turned around, looking for the Queen. "My dear!" he called. "Have this cat removed."

"Off with his head!" shouted the Queen, without even turning round.

However, the executioner insisted that in order for a head to be removed, there had to be a body attached to it. Since the Cheshire Cat was only a head, there was no way of chopping it off.

"That Cat belongs to the Duchess," Alice said. "Perhaps she can solve the problem."

"Fetch the Duchess!" the Queen told the Cheshire Cat, and he disappeared.

The Mock Turtle's Story

Suddenly, the Duchess appeared as if from nowhere. "I'm so glad to see you!" she cried, greeting Alice as if she were an old friend. Alice was pleased that she was in a better mood now than she had been the last time they met!

The Duchess tucked her arm into Alice's, and the two walked off together. But after just a short time, Alice began to feel quite uncomfortable. The Duchess was exactly the right height to rest her chin on Alice's shoulder. It was a very pointy little chin, and it dug into Alice's shoulder painfully. Alice didn't want to be rude, so she put up with it as best she could.

As they walked along, the Duchess grew very talkative, repeating old sayings like, "Love makes the world go round!" and "Birds of a feather flock together!" Alice was growing bored, but every time her attention drifted, the Duchess pushed her sharp, pointy chin into Alice's shoulder to bring her back.

All at once, though, the Duchess's voice died away, right in the middle of a word, and Alice felt her begin to tremble. Looking up, Alice saw that the Queen was standing right in front of them.

"A fine day, your Majesty!" said the Duchess, softly.

The Queen stamped her foot angrily. "I'm giving you fair warning," she said to the Duchess. "Either you or your head must be off! Take your choice!"

The Duchess was gone in a flash.

"Now," said the Queen, "have you met the Mock Turtle yet?"

"I didn't even know there was such a thing as a Mock Turtle," Alice replied.

"Of course there is!" said the Queen. "What do you think Mock Turtle soup is made from?"

Alice and the Queen came upon the Gryphon, a strange beast unlike anything Alice had ever seen before. He was lying fast asleep in the sunshine.

"Get up, you lazy thing!" ordered the Queen. "Take this young lady to see the Mock Turtle so he can tell her his story. I must go and see about some executions."

The Gryphon sat up, rubbed his eyes, and watched till the Queen was out of sight. "It's all her fancy, you know," he told Alice. "They never execute anyone!"

They set off together, and soon found the Mock Turtle sitting on a rock and looking sad and lonely.

"This young lady wants to hear your story," the Gryphon told him.

So the Mock Turtle began. "I was a real Turtle," he said. "When I was little, I went to school in the sea with the other little Turtles. We had ten hours of lessons a day – everything you need to learn."

"I've been to school, too," said Alice.

"Did you learn washing?" asked the Mock Turtle.

"Certainly not!" cried Alice.

"That's enough about the lessons," the Gryphon interrupted. "Now tell her about the games!"

The Lobster Quadrille

"I will tell you about the Lobster Quadrille," the Mock Turtle told Alice. "Have you ever seen it?"

"No, I haven't," said Alice. "What sort of dance is it?" She was very interested to find out.

"There are lines," replied the Mock Turtle. "Seals, turtles, salmon on one side, each with a lobster partner on the other side."

"It must be very pretty," Alice remarked.

"Would you like to see it? We can do it without the lobsters! Come," the Mock Turtle said to the Gryphon, "let's do the first figure. I'll sing."

So they began solemnly dancing, while the Mock Turtle sang, very sadly, a beautiful song that ended with:

"Will you, won't you, will you, won't you, won't you join the dance?"

"Now," said the Gryphon to Alice, "you tell us some of your adventures."

So Alice told them about all the things that had happened to her that day, beginning with when she first saw the White Rabbit.

When she had finished, the Mock Turtle drew a long breath and said, "That's very curious."

He had just begun singing another song when a loud cry came from the distance:

"The trial's beginning!"

"Come on!" shouted the Gryphon, grabbing Alice's hand. "We have to hurry!"

Alice and the Gryphon arrived in the courtroom to find the King and Queen of Hearts sitting on their thrones. The room was filled with what looked like a whole pack of playing cards, and the jury box was filled with animals who were holding slates and pencils.

As the King was also the judge, he wore his crown over a judge's wig. Next to him stood the White Rabbit, holding a trumpet in one hand and a parchment scroll in the other. The jury consisted of twelve different creatures, all busily writing on slates.

Alice sat down next to the Dormouse, right behind the jury box. She noticed a plate of tarts on a table in the middle of the courtroom. She hoped that they would be served as refreshments. But the tarts were not refreshments – they were evidence. The Knave of Hearts was accused of stealing them, and he stood at the front of the courtroom, bound in chains and guarded by two soldiers.

"Herald, read the accusation," ordered the King.

The White Rabbit blew three blasts on the trumpet, unrolled the parchment scroll and read:

"The Queen of Hearts, she made some tarts,
All on a summer's day.
The Knave of Hearts, he stole those tarts,
And took them quite away!"

The first witness to be called was the Hatter. As he gave his evidence, Alice began to get a strange feeling. At the same time, the Dormouse began to fidget.

"I wish you wouldn't squeeze that way," the Dormouse said to Alice. "I can hardly breathe!"

"I can't help it," Alice replied. "I'm growing!"

"Well, you've got no right at all to grow here!" said the Dormouse crossly.

"You're growing too, you know!" said Alice.

"Not as ridiculously fast as you!" said the Dormouse, With a huff, he got up and went to sit somewhere else.

Meanwhile, the Hatter had finished giving his evidence, and the next witness was called in. Even before she entered the room, people near the door began sneezing. Alice guessed that the witness must be the Duchess's cook, with her pepper-pot, and she was right.

The cook walked in and took a seat in the witness box. But she did not have much to say, so it was soon time for the next witness. At the top of his shrill little voice, the White Rabbit called, "Alice!"

"Here!" cried Alice, jumping up in such a hurry that she knocked over the jury box – for she had by now grown quite tall.

"The trial cannot continue," said the King, "until all the jurors are back in their proper places."

So Alice had to stop and pick up all the little creatures and make sure they were back where they belonged. She picked up their slates and pencils, too.

Finally she made her way to the witness box.

Alice's Evidence

"What do you know about all this business?" the King asked Alice.

"Nothing," said Alice.

"Nothing whatever?" persisted the King.

"Nothing whatever," said Alice.

The King was busy writing in his notebook as well. When he had finished, he read out: "Rule Forty-two: all persons more than a mile high are to leave the court."

Everyone looked at Alice.

"I'm not a mile high," she protested.

"You are," said the King.

"Nearly two miles high, in fact," added the Queen.

"Well, I won't go," said Alice. "Besides, that's not a real rule. You invented it just now."

"It's the oldest rule in the book!" the King insisted.

"Then it should be Rule One!" Alice shouted.

The King turned pale and slammed his notebook shut.

"Silence!" he cried.

"Hold your tongue!" ordered the Queen.

"I won't!" said Alice defiantly. She had grown so tall now that she wasn't afraid of anyone in the courtroom.

"Off with her head!" the Queen screeched.

"Who cares about you?" Alice shouted back at her. She had grown to her full size now, and towered over everyone. "You're nothing but a pack of cards!"

At this, the whole pack flew up in the air and began to tumble down over her...

Alice gave a little scream, half of fright and half of anger, and tried to beat off the cards.

"Wake up, Alice dear," said a voice – a kind and familiar voice.

Alice opened her eyes and found herself back at the riverbank, looking up at her sister, who was brushing away some leaves that had fluttered down and fallen on Alice's face.

"What a long sleep you've had," said her sister.

"Oh!" said Alice, sitting up. "I've had the most curious dream!"

And she told her sister, as well as she could remember them, of all the strange and amazing things that had happened to her.

And when she had finished, her sister kissed her, and said, "It was a curious dream, but now run in to have your tea. It's getting late."

And Alice ran off, thinking of what a wonderful dream it had been, but happy to be going home.

Her sister sat watching her go in the setting sun, and leant her head on her hand. She thought about all the remarkable things Alice had told her. And she thought about how her little sister would someday be a grown-up woman, with children of her own. And she hoped that when she did grow up, Alice would remember the marvellous stories of Wonderland, and the happiness of her childhood summer days.

About the author

Lewis Carroll's real name was Charles Lutwidge Dodgson. He was born in 1832 in Cheshire, England. Lewis was schooled at home until he was 12, and then went to Rugby School in Warwickshire, and then to Christ Church College, Oxford, where he studied mathematics. He became a lecturer in mathematics at Oxford University after he graduated. Lewis had no children of his own, but he enjoyed telling stories to his friends' children, who loved to hear about Alice's strange encounters in a magical land. The original story of *Alice's Adventures in Wonderland* was first published in 1865. Lewis continued telling stories into his last years, and died in 1898 at his sister's home in Surrey.

Other titles in the Classic Collection series:

Editor: Lauren Taylor • Designer: Izzy Langridge • Cover typography: Matthew Kelly

Copyright © QED Publishing 2011

First published in the UK in 2011 by
QED Publishing, A Quarto Group company,
226 City Road, London EC1V 2TT

www.qed-publishing.co.uk

A catalogue record for this book is available from the British Library.

ISBN 978 1 84835 550 7

Printed in China